The Pirate
and the
Penguin

Written and Illustrated by Patricia Storms

For my Guido, who is always reminding me that "it really doesn't matter if
I'm wrong, I'm right where I belong."
And for Liam, with much gratitude.

Owlkids Books Inc.
10 Lower Spadina Avenue, Suite 400, Toronto, Ontario M5V 2Z2
www.owlkids.com

Distributed in Canada by Raincoast Books
9050 Shaughnessy Street, Vancouver, British Columbia V6P 6E5

Distributed in the United States by Publishers Group West
1700 Fourth Street, Berkeley, California 94710

Library and Archives Canada Cataloguing in Publication
Storms, Patricia
The pirate and the penguin / Patricia Storms.
ISBN 978-1-897349-67-0
1. Penguins--Juvenile fiction. I. Title.

PS8637.T6755P75 2009   jC813'.6   C2009-900999-4

Library of Congress Control Number: 2009923342

Design: Barb Kelly

Canada Council   Conseil des Arts   ONTARIO ARTS COUNCIL
for the Arts   du Canada   CONSEIL DES ARTS DE L'ONTARIO

We acknowledge the financial support of the Canada Council for the Arts, the Ontario Arts Council, the Government of Canada
through the Book Publishing Industry Development Program (BPIDP), and the Government of Ontario through the Ontario Media
Development Corporation's Book Initiative for our publishing activities.

Printed in China

A   B   C   D   E   F

Publisher of Chirp, chickaDEE and OWL
www.owlkids.com

"Why are you knitting a sweater?" asked Penguin's friends.

"Because the South Pole is too cold!" said Penguin with a shudder. "Besides, there's nothing to do here!"

"But there's so much to do.
Like daydreaming!"

"And yoga!"

"And daydreaming *about* yoga!"

"Don't you want to do more than just sit around and think?" said Penguin. "I have itchy feet!"

"I want to see what's beyond this big boring block of ice."

WHUMP!

"What are you doing?" asked Penguin.

"You said you had itchy feet," said his friends.

"That's not what I meant!" Penguin shouted.

"I'm tired of being bored and cold!" yelled Penguin.

"I'm off to find adventure and sunshine!"

Many miles away, in the Caribbean Sea, there was a pirate. Well, there were lots of pirates, but this one was different.

"Captain, why don't you like this beautiful sunshine?" asked his crew.

"Sailing somewhere will cheer you up," said the first mate.

"I'd rather set anchor and relax," said Pirate.

"But Captain," said the crew, "if we don't go anywhere, we won't find any treasure."

tHis eNd uP matey

"What's so great about finding treasure?" sighed Pirate. "I'd just like to find inner peace."

"Inner peace?" asked the crew.
"Is that on one of our treasure maps?"

"If you want to find treasure that badly," said Pirate, "then YOU steer the ship!

I'm going down to my cabin!"

Inside his cabin, it was cool and quiet.
Very slowly, Pirate fell asleep.

While Pirate slept, the crew began to sail off course.

And where was Penguin going?

Pirate was just waking up from his nap when...

"Wow!" said Penguin.
"Am I on a REAL pirate ship?"

"Yes, you are, you trespasser!" said Pirate.
"And pirates make trespassers walk the plank!"

drag drag

"Okay, okay," said Penguin. "But before I walk the plank, may I have one final wish? May I try on your hat? I've always wanted to be a pirate."

"Well, it is your final wish," said Pirate. "Come off the plank, but only for a minute."

"Are you still going to make me walk the plank?" asked Penguin, showing his very best pirate grin. "Because you don't seem like a very nasty pirate."

"You're right," sighed Pirate. "I'm tired of being nasty." Then he smiled, "That hat really suits you. Why don't you try on my coat, too."

"Okay!" said Penguin. "And you try on my sweater!"

"Penguins don't actually *QUACK*, you know," giggled Penguin.

"And pirates don't usually say *GRRRRRR!*" laughed Pirate.

Just then the crew raced over in a panic. "Captain, we're lost!" cried the first mate. "HEY! Which one of you is our Captain?"

Pirate had an idea. He winked at Penguin.

"Please," he said, "I'm just a poor, lost penguin who wants to go home!"

"I think we could let him go...this time!" said Penguin.

"Do you think your crew will believe that I'm their captain?" whispered Penguin.

"Oh, they'll love you!" said Pirate. "And maybe your friends will think I'm a penguin!"

So Penguin led Pirate's crew around the world, finding treasure along the way and eating lots of exotic fruits. He never felt bored or cold again.

And Pirate? He paddled to the South Pole.

"You're back?" asked Penguin's friends.
"You said you had itchy feet."

But Pirate wasn't itchy anymore.
For the first time, he felt right at home.